The FIREFIGHTERS' THANKSGIVING

by **MARIBETH BOELTS**   illustrated by **TERRY WIDENER**

To all firefighters,
Waterloo Fire Rescue,
Darwin and Mick. —M. B.

For L.S.W. (25) —T. W.

Text copyright © 2004 by Maribeth Boelts.

Illustrations copyright © 2004 by Terry Widener.

All rights reserved. This book, or parts thereof, may not

be reproduced in any form without permission in writing from

the publisher, G. P. Putnam's Sons, a division of Penguin Young

Readers Group, 345 Hudson Street, New York, NY 10014.

G. P. Putnam's Sons, Reg. U.S. Pat. & Tm. Off.

The scanning, uploading and distribution of this

book via the Internet or via any other means

without the permission of the publisher is illegal

and punishable by law. Please purchase only

authorized electronic editions, and do not participate

in or encourage electronic piracy of copyrighted materials.

Your support of the author's rights is appreciated.

Published simultaneously in Canada.

Manufactured in China by South China Printing Co. Ltd.

Designed by Gunta Alexander. Text set in Sodium.

The art was done in Golden acrylics on Strathmore paper.

Library of Congress Cataloging-in-Publication Data

The firefighters' Thanksgiving / by Maribeth Boelts;

illustrated by Terry Widener. p. cm.

Summary: Calls to fires, an injured friend, and

cooking disasters threaten to keep a group of fire

fighters from enjoying Thanksgiving dinner.

[1. Fire fighters—Fiction. 2. Thanksgiving Day—Fiction. 3.

Stories in rhyme.] I. Widener, Terry, ill. II. Title. PZ8.3.B599545

Fi 2004 [E]—dc21 00-045909 ISBN 0-399-23600-7

10 9 8 7 6 5 4 3 2 1   First Impression

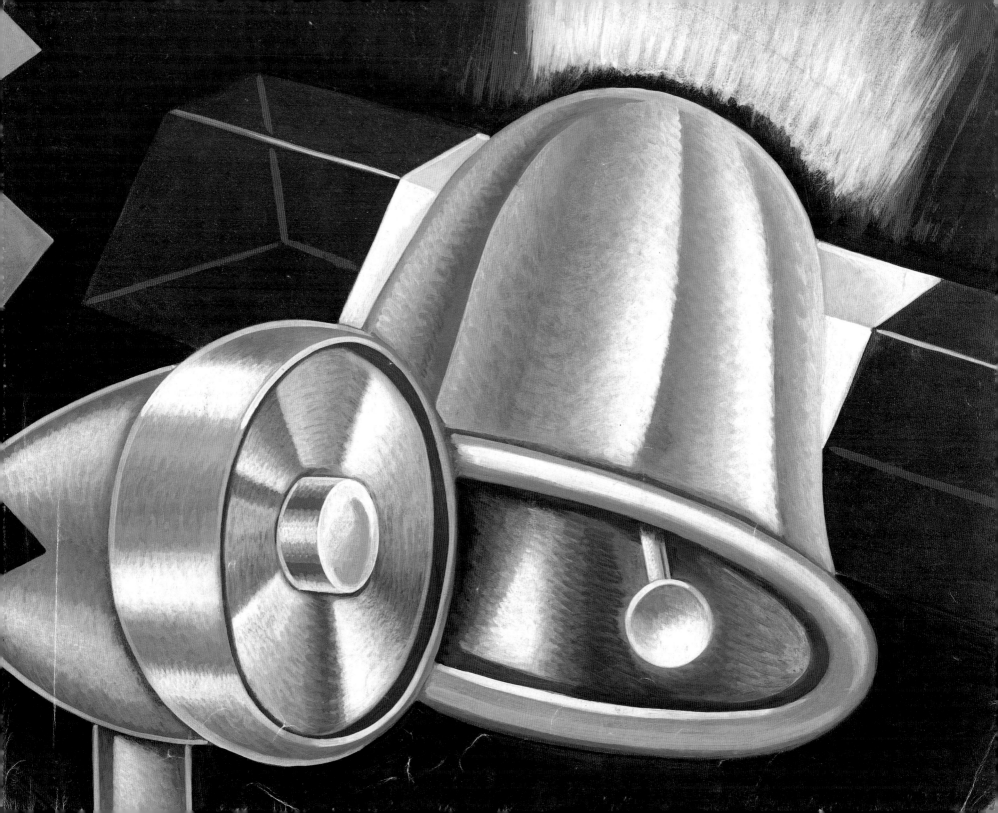

Thanksgiving Day—this shift's begun.
Ten firefighters at Station 1.

Lou says, "I can cook today."
A list is made. They're on their way.

A turkey, pumpkin, yeast, potatoes,
ice cream, yams and ripe tomatoes.
The cart is full, the shopping's through.

A call comes in—it's 9:02.

Sooty, smoky, back to the store.
They help mop ice cream from the floor.
They split the tab, then peel and clean.

A call comes in—it's 12:15.

They wash the trucks, hang hose to dry.

Roll out crust for pumpkin pie.

Pack up gear and fill the tank.

Plan the next big rookie prank.

The turkey's frozen. Is it too late?

A call comes in—it's 2:08.

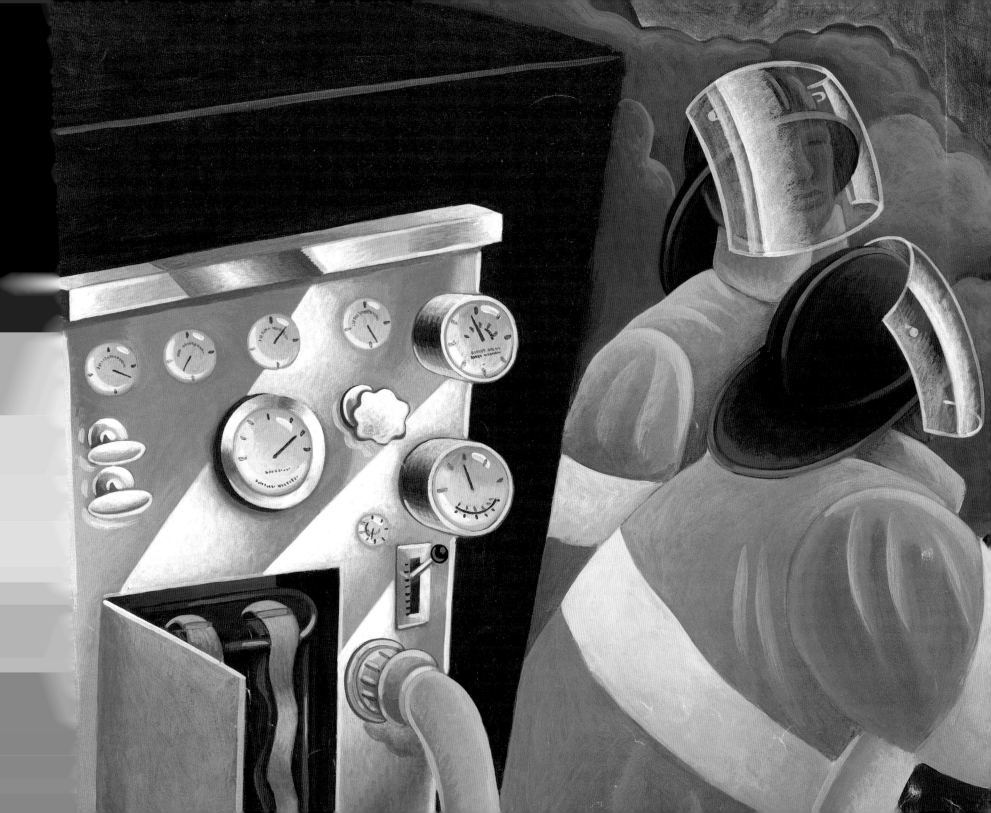

They check equipment, fix a tire.

Record the details of the fire.

Put potatoes on to boil.

Refuel the trucks and change the oil.

Throw out pie crust, start again.

A call comes in—it's 4:10.

Lou is hurt! Firefighters worry.

To the hospital in a hurry.

The meal forgotten, some pace, some pray.

They get the news . . .

He'll be okay.

Back at the station, night is falling.
Families will soon be calling.
The turkey's raw, the potatoes, too.
No pies, no bread, just thoughts of Lou.
They wash the trucks and hose the floor.

A call comes in—it's 8:04.

While they fight fires,
a feast is spread—
Turkey, stuffing, pies and bread.
A note is on the table, too: